SUPER FLY

FLY

Revenge
of the
Roach!

The Super Fly series

The World's Smallest Superhero!

Revenge of the Roach!

Super Fly vs. Furious Flea!
(coming soon)

SUPER FLY

Revenge of the Roach!

Todd H. Doodler

BLOOMSBURY

NEW YORK   LONDON   OXFORD   NEW DELHI   SYDNEY

First published in the United States of America in June 2016
by Bloomsbury Children's Books
www.bloomsbury.com

Bloomsbury is a registered trademark of Bloomsbury Publishing Plc

For information about permission to reproduce selections from this book, write to
Permissions, Bloomsbury Children's Books, 1385 Broadway, New York, New York 10018
Bloomsbury books may be purchased for business or promotional use. For information on bulk
purchases please contact Macmillan Corporate and Premium Sales Department at
specialmarkets@macmillan.com

Library of Congress Cataloging-in-Publication Data
Names: Doodler, Todd H., author, illustrator.
Title: Super Fly! : revenge of the roach! / by Todd H. Doodler.
Other titles: Revenge of the roach
Description: New York : Bloomsbury, 2016. | Series: Super Fly
Summary: When Crazy Cockroach and two dung beetle henchmen try to brainwash the
children of Stinkopolis using video games, only Super Fly and his sidekick, Fantastic Flea,
can stop them.
Identifiers: LCCN 2015037950
ISBN 978-1-61963-381-0 (paperback) • ISBN 978-1-61963-382-7 (hardcover)
ISBN 978-1-61963-383-4 (e-book)
Subjects: | CYAC: Superheroes—Fiction. | Flies—Fiction. | Insects—Fiction. | Video
games—Fiction. | Brainwashing—Fiction. | BISAC: JUVENILE FICTION/Humorous
Stories. | JUVENILE FICTION/Action & Adventure/General. | JUVENILE FICTION/
Comics & Graphic Novels/ Superheroes.
Classification: LCC PZ7.D7247 Sr 2016 | DDC [Fic]—dc23
LC record available at https://lccn.loc.gov/2015037950

Book design by Nicole Gastonguay and Yelena Safronova
Printed and bound in the U.S.A. by Berryville Graphics Inc., Berryville, Virginia
2 4 6 8 10 9 7 5 3 1

All papers used by Bloomsbury Publishing, Inc., are natural, recyclable products
made from wood grown in well-managed forests. The manufacturing processes
conform to the environmental regulations of the country of origin.

To my daughter, Elle—you will always be my FLY GIRL!

CONTENTS

1. Super Pie 1

2. Return of the Roach 14

3. Number 1 and Number 2 29

4. The Big Bad Bully Bug Is Back . . . 38

5. The Pizza Guy Is a Pizza Fly 49

6. Operation Super Spy 58

7. Crazy Cockroach Says! 63

8. The Technology Trap 69

9. King of the School 73

10. Cornelius for Mayor 77

11. Roach Domination 85

12. The Big Contest 90

13. Fly Girl 98

14. Reverse Engineering 102

15. Three on Three 112

1

Super Pie

Eugene Flystein and his friend Fred Flea were ordinary fourth graders. Or so it seemed to most of the bugs living in Stinkopolis, a town located in the stinkiest part of an extremely stinky city dump.

Most students at Brown Barge Elementary School thought Eugene was a nerd. They'd seen him get slammed in dodgeball. What fly can't fly?

And one look at Eugene flailing and then failing to catch a fly ball was enough to earn him the nerd word for life.

But lately his younger sister, Elle, had seen flashes of a different Eugene. Something big had happened to her

beloved brother. The clever second grader didn't know what—yet. She would find out!

So one day after school, Elle spied on Eugene and Fred. It wasn't the exciting kind of spying with fake identities, laser guns, and night-vision goggles. She just watched and listened without letting them know.

Eugene looked inside the fridge and groaned. "I'm so hungry, I could eat a flower!"

Fred shuddered. "Ew! I thought flowers were your kryptonite."

Eugene looked around the kitchen. Elle ducked out of view just in time!

She knew kryptonite was the stuff that made some superheroes weak. What could that have to do with her brother—unless her wildest suspicions were right?

Eugene took out a big plate and inhaled a mixture of oozing odors. "Ah! Want some of last night's poo-poo platter?"

Fred refused. "Thanks, but I bit a really fat dog for lunch."

Eugene rubbed his forelegs eagerly. "Great! More for me."

While Eugene stuffed his mouth parts, Fred asked, "So . . . do you want to practice today, or see if we can reach the next level of *Sewer Invaders*?"

Eugene briefly stopped eating. "I suppose we should practice, but . . ."

Fred interrupted. "I have some new moves I'd like to try."

Eugene grinned. "Me too! Let's practice tomorrow."

Fred held up a leg. Eugene met the salute with the tip of one wing. "High *flyve*! Let's play!"

While the boys played *Sewer Invaders*,

4

Elle slipped quietly into the kitchen. What could her brother and his pint-size friend think they should be practicing? Was Fred teaching Eugene circus tricks so he could perform with Fred's family?

Elle opened the refrigerator. She was more curious than hungry. She'd seen that key lime pie before. On the first day of school, when all that strange stuff happened.

Now signs covered the pale-green pie.

Elle considered eating it. With all those warnings, her big brother was practically begging her to.

Elle wasn't sure what *peligroso* meant. The *gross* part sounded yummy. But wasn't *peligroso* the Spanish word for dangerous? How could pie be dangerous?

"**HIGH FLYVE!**" The boys' noisy cheer echoed through the Flysteins' kitchen.

Eugene shouted, "Next level!"

Fred exclaimed, "Doody calls!"

Eugene looked skeptical. "Really? Is that what you're saying now?"

Fred asked, "Don't you think it's cool?"

Eugene considered. "Maybe . . . it's totally awesome! We should save it for missions."

Fred turned a few somersaults in the air. Elle almost clapped. She loved when Fred performed circus tricks!

For the moment, Elle forgot the mystery of the key lime pie. Instead she wondered, *Missions? What kind of missions involve a fourth grader and his best friend?*

The boys suddenly turned around. Eugene stammered, "Elle! We . . . made it to level two."

"Congrats." Elle searched her brother's face. His eyes hid behind his thick glasses.

Elle sighed. She loved Eugene, but sometimes even she had to admit he was a nerd.

"Whatever." Elle closed the refrigerator. "Catch you later."

"Said the spider to the fly," Eugene teased.

Elle shuddered.

Eugene quickly apologized. "I'm sorry!"

"It's okay," Elle assured him. "I'm a big bug now. I won't have nightmares."

Eugene hesitated. The Ultimo 6-9000 (patent pending) had increased all his powers by 9,000 times in just six seconds. Sure, it looked exactly like an ordinary if somewhat pathetic slice of key lime pie, but that pie turned a nerd into Super Fly— among other amazing things.

The brilliant bug suspected that his sister suspected something.

Elle asked, "Any poo-poo platter left?"

Eugene smiled. "I saved the best poo for you."

Elle gave him a quick hug. "You're the best brother ever!"

Then, since Elle's forelegs were full of the foully fragrant platter, she asked, "Can you please open my door?"

Eugene reached for the knob and . . . ripped the door to Elle's room right off its hinges!

Fred muttered, "Not again!"

On the first day he'd become Super Fly, Eugene tore off the Flysteins' front door. Luckily it only took about eleven seconds for Super Fly to fly all over the dump, find a door just like it, and put the door back up.

No one seemed to notice the different door. Eugene hoped he could fix Elle's door before too many questions were asked.

"Oops!" he exclaimed. "Guess I don't know my own strength."

Fred added hastily, "We've been working out."

Elle looked each boy in the eyes. "You've been playing *Sewer Invaders*."

"You know how many muscles you use controlling a joystick?" Eugene said while flexing his almost nonexistent muscles.

Fred hopped from foot to foot to foot nervously. "Yeah, well. Speaking of which, we have level two to do."

2

Return of the Roach

Eugene wasn't the only one acting strange in Stinkopolis. The next day at Brown Barge Elementary School, a surprising silhouette darkened Mrs. Tiger Moth's classroom door.

With senses 9,000 times greater than the average fly's already amazing senses, Eugene felt a tingling in his danger receptor. He wasn't sure where this receptor was, but he knew that all superheroes have one since they're pretty much always in danger.

Eugene took off his thick glasses so he could examine the new arrival with Super Fly's eyes. He blinked at the tall, shadowy figure. It couldn't be . . . but it was!

Super Fly's archenemy, the very villain who had forced him to become a hero.

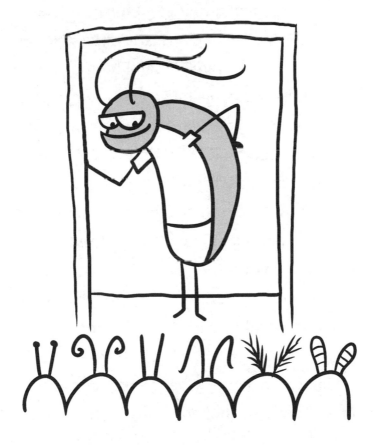

Cornelius C. Roach, the worst bully Brown Barge Elementary School had ever known, was now the super villain Crazy Cockroach.

Somehow this evil fiend had escaped a lunar deathtrap and returned to Mrs. Tiger Moth's class.

Eugene turned to look at his pest friend.

Fred shrugged. Fantastic Flea had no more of a clue than Super Fly about how Cornelius could be back at Brown Barge. Who would expect a cockroach stranded under a huge rock **ON THE MOON** to walk through the classroom door?

Mrs. Tiger Moth fluttered her wings in surprise and exclaimed, "Cornelius! It's . . . nice to see you."

Her words were more polite than true. Even the kindly teacher hadn't missed the nasty bully.

Like everyone else at Brown Barge, Mrs. Tiger Moth had enjoyed living in a

Cornelius-free world. Lunch money actually bought lunches. No one came back from recess with bruised eyes or broken feelers. And bugs really did their own homework.

Then just when they'd all gotten used to school being a safe place, even for nerds, the roach returned.

Mrs. Tiger Moth asked, "Were you sick?"

Cornelius smiled and said, "No thanks. I'll have a cheesebooger, hold the boogers."

Mrs. Tiger Moth's wings fluttered again. "Cornelius? I asked if you've been sick."

Cornelius didn't reply. Instead, he danced down the aisle between the first two rows of chairs.

Eugene cringed as the bully pranced past his chair, waving his antennae wildly to a beat no other bug heard.

Fred scribbled a note to Eugene.

In milliseconds, Super Fly's super eyes read the words.

Space fever?

Super Fly regarded his enemy. Was this really the same roach he'd flown to the moon in order to save Earth?

Cornelius babbled to his pencil. "Listen, lead

head, I'm not the crazy one. You're the one who can't stop skateboarding on the ceiling."

Cornelius tilted his antennae, as if listening to the pencil's side of the argument. Whatever he heard made Cornelius so mad he zipped the pencil into his pencil case and slammed the case inside his desk.

Then the ranting roach opened his math book. Cornelius licked a page and muttered, "Long division—how delicious!"

Mrs. Tiger Moth made a quick note in her grade book, then she forced herself to smile. "Yes, Cornelius, delicious. Now, who would like to eat—I mean, answer—the first question?"

Cornelius eagerly answered. Unfortunately his response made even less sense than his request for a "cheesebooger, hold the boogers."

Cornelius's behavior stayed strange all morning. He never said a mean word! When nervous laughter greeted some of his weird answers, Cornelius didn't squash the laughers. Instead, he joined them.

Everyone at Brown Barge always gave the roach plenty of room to swagger down the halls. As students scurried away from him, the big roach seemed puzzled.

Eugene whispered, "Why isn't he tripping anyone?"

Fred shrugged. "Do you think he's actually going to pay for his own lunch?"

"He hasn't locked a single bug in a locker yet! Something's not right," muttered Eugene.

Eugene took off his glasses and looked

Fred directly in the eyes. "I'm going to find out."

Ever since that first day of school when Cornelius called Fred everything except his name, Fred had disliked Cornelius. Now that the bully was 9,000 times stronger and meaner, Fred disliked him 9,000 times as much.

As a loyal sidekick, Fantastic Flea would leap into battle if Super Fly needed him. He just hoped that wouldn't happen.

Super Fly began with a direct question. "You don't seem like yourself, Cornelius. Are you okay?"

"I'm butterscotch

Wednesday!" the cockroach exclaimed. He tossed an imaginary ball in the air, caught it several times, then dropped it and scurried down the hall, chasing it and screaming, "Come back, Mr. Pancake!"

Super Fly and Fred hurried after the bizarre bug. Fred asked, "Do you think he's dangerous?"

Cornelius suddenly stopped running and stood on his head.

Eugene whispered, "I guess he's no more dangerous than usual."

Considering that "usual" for Crazy Cockroach included trying to take over the world with giant robots, that didn't comfort Fred.

For the rest of the day, Super Fly and Fantastic Flea kept their eyes on Cornelius. He really *did* pay for his own lunch! Cornelius drank the mustard like a smoothie and slurped moldy spaghetti mixed with pencil shavings and dust bunnies for dessert.

When the braver boys laughed at Cornelius's mustard mustache, he laughed too! Then Cornelius put on a bigger mustache and jumped from table to table until the period ended.

He thanked the lunch lady for a lovely dance and wished her a happy New Year. Cornelius spent recess playing with an

invisible yoyo and jumping over an equally invisible rope.

On the bus home from school, Cornelius licked more pages in his math book and stuck his head out the window like a dog. Then he shouted, "Who wants to make up songs?"

Without waiting for an answer, Cornelius commenced loudly singing to the tune of *I'm a little teapot, short and stout*: "I'm a giant cockroach, tall and brown. Here are my feelers; where is my crown?"

Elle leaned forward in her seat to hear what Eugene said to Fred. "Do you think he left his marbles on the moon?"

"What marbles?" Fred replied.

Eugene sighed. "It's just an expression that means do you think Cornelius has lost his mind?"

Elle wondered if her brother had lost

his. She asked, "What does Cornelius have to do with the moon?"

Eugene pushed his glasses back up and looked nervous. "Moon? What moon?"

Elle said, "The one in the sky."

"Yeah, right, that moon," Fred babbled. "That's just an expression too. Cornelius couldn't have been to the moon. He's just an ordinary cockroach who's started licking his math book for no reason, especially not space fever."

Eugene reached over and closed Fred's mouth. The flea managed to murmur, "Thank you."

Luckily at that exact moment Cornelius pulled down his pants and mooned the entire bus.

"No, we meant *that* moon," Eugene said to his sister, pointing at Cornelius's surprisingly tanned behind.

Elle wasn't buying it.

On the way home from the bus stop, Elle trotted to catch up to the boys. "What's all the fuss? So Cornelius is acting weird. So what? Weird is better than how mean he usually is."

Eugene shrugged. "It's just strange."

Fred echoed, "We like to investigate strange things." Then he added, "Just because. It's not like we're superheroes or anything."

Elle looked surprised as Eugene once again shut his pest friend's mouth. Fred murmured, "Sorry. Thanks. Really sorry."

Elle would get to bottom of this.

3

Number 1 and Number 2

The next morning at Brown Barge Elementary, Eugene, Fred, and Elle stepped off the bus into chaos. A swarm of gnats flew around the bus platform, buzzing in terror.

The tiny gnats kept bumping into each other, which made them even more scared, so they flew faster and . . .

"Gnats strange! Wonder what's got them all stirred up?" Eugene asked.

Fred spotted two nasty dung beetles waving their antennae and rushing at the swarm of terrified gnats. Fred knew these troublemaker twin brothers, big beetles named Dee and Doo Dung.

Lucy Kaboosie, a brave ladybug, dared to defy the mean twins. "You should pick on bugs your own size!"

Dee and Doo turned to Lucy. Her polka-dotted wing covers rustled nervously.

Eugene reached for his eyeglasses. If he had to protect the mayor's beautiful daughter, Eugene wouldn't hesitate to turn into Super Fly—even in front of the whole school.

But the dastardly Dungs didn't attack lovely Lucy, because just then, Cornelius strolled by.

As he slowly licked the pages, Cornelius again sang to himself, "I'm a giant cockroach, tall and brown. Here are my feelers. Where is my crown?"

Dee and Doo stared at the roach. Then they turned to each other and burst out laughing.

The beetles walked on either side of Cornelius, taking turns trying to trip him and grab his feelers.

Cornelius looked confused. "Why are you interrupting my song?"

Dee kneeled down behind Cornelius, and then Doo pushed the roach so he fell backward over Dee. As Cornelius struggled to regain his footing, they laughed louder and louder.

Super Fly's danger receptor tingled. How much longer would the big roach take the twins' teasing?

Fantastic Flea whispered, "Should we help him?"

Hero and sidekick wondered: Was it wrong to just stand by while a bully was bullied?

Before Super Fly could help the roach stand up, Cornelius made it to his feet on his own.

The twins instantly tipped the riled roach onto his back. As Cornelius's legs wiggled in the air, they laughed even louder.

Even bugs without a danger receptor felt the tension as Cornelius continued to struggle.

Then Cornelius snapped to his feet. Something had changed. The confused amateur singer suddenly looked fearless and fierce!

Faster than lightning, Cornelius grabbed both beetles and bent their heads under his forefeet.

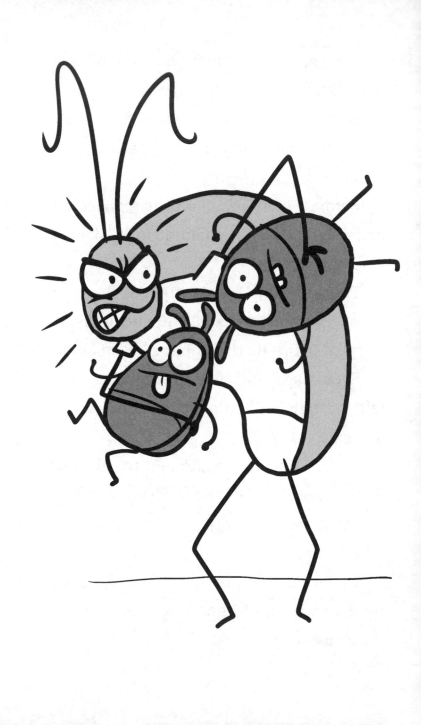

The stinkbug standing near Eugene released a puff of stinky gas. Eugene guessed the crazed cockroach's armpits smelled even worse. The captive Dungs certainly seemed to think so.

Fred flinched. "How can a black bug turn lime green?" he asked.

Eugene shrugged. The stench rising from Cornelius's pits seemed capable of anything.

Cornelius cackled with cruel pride. "I'm back, you helpless larvae! I'm back to claim my kingdom. King of the cockroaches and therefore king of the world!"

Dee gasped. "Okay, you're . . . the king!"

"Ruler of the world. Just let us . . . go!" Doo begged.

Cornelius lifted his forelegs in triumph, and the twins dropped to the ground. He laughed. "You two will make great henchbugs. I will call you Number 1 and Number 2."

Dee and Doo had no choice—unless they wanted to risk death by armpit. They'd both felt Cornelius's surprising power. Clearly Cornelius had become much more than an ordinary school-yard bully.

The beetles were moving up, from school yards to . . . the Dungs didn't know yet. They would follow Cornelius and find out. As Henchbugs Number 1 and Number 2, the miserable twins caught a glimpse of something they'd never known: purpose.

The Big Bad Bully Bug
Is Back

After school Cornelius led his henchbugs to his new lair. As the Dungs crawled inside, the roach explained, "It's part secret lab, part clubhouse. As my henchbugs, you'll have access to the Ping-Pong table, the fridge, and the gym I'm planning to build."

Doo exclaimed, "All this in an old diaper. Enchanting smell!"

Dee agreed, "You built an impressive lair. But that doesn't make you a super villain."

Anger made the cockroach roar, "How

many times must I tell you dim Dungs: **I AM CRAZY COCKROACH, THE SUPER VILLAIN WHO TRIED TO TAKE OVER THE WORLD WITH GIANT ROBOTS!**"

Dee looked stunned. "You're so loud!"

Doo snickered. "Okay, you're bad. But *Crazy Cockroach* bad? No way!"

Dee went on, "That bad bug was on TV, bro. Real, *live* TV."

While the twins scoffed, Cornelius slipped behind a curtain. He emerged dressed as . . . Crazy Cockroach!

Doo applauded. "Nice costume. It's almost real."

Dee added, "Those Halloween companies sure don't waste any time."

Cornelius fumed. What would it take to convince these dumb Dungs? Crazy Cockroach tossed the twins to the top of the diaper and juggled them till they puked.

"Gack!" Doo protested. "That just proves you're mean."

Dee stepped around a puddle. "And that you don't mind housework. Because I am *not* cleaning that up."

Crazy Cockroach twirled his hands at top speed. He spun so fast that puke particles swirled up around him.

The Dungs rushed outside before the growing

puke vortex could suck them in. They cowered behind a rusted cat food can to watch Cornelius wrap the puke ball in a scrap of diaper and then soar out of his lair.

The beetles looked up. Against the bright-blue sky flew the super villain known as Crazy Cockroach. He tossed the puke ball so far, so fast, it ignited like a meteor and rained onto a distant suburb.

Then they heard strange noises coming from the far side of the diaper. The Dungs rushed back into Cornelius's lair.

Dee asked, "What was that?"

Doo's feelers wiggled to form two question marks.

Crazy Cockroach swooped into the diaper. "Are you dull-witted Dungs ready to admit I am indeed the super villain Crazy Cockroach?"

"Shh!" Dee hissed.

"Something's happening on the other side of the diaper," Doo whispered.

Thanks to his super hearing, Crazy Cockroach heard every grunt and rustle. Then a familiar voice said, "Almost. Try again."

Grunt, rustle.

Cornelius rushed outside with his henchbugs behind him.

The diaper had another leg hole, another entrance.

The moment he crawled onto its soggy cotton floor, Crazy Cockroach recognized his archenemy. Super Fly was practicing cool-looking thorax kicks with Fantastic Flea!

On the next move, the tip of Eugene's leg grazed his practice partner. Fred flipped over and over and over, reeling from the momentum of Super Fly's super kick.

Eugene exclaimed, "Sorry!"

"It's okay," Fred replied. "Ask any dog: fleas are tough!"

Then, superhero and sidekick had the same thought at the same moment: *We are not alone!* They turned and saw Crazy Cockroach and his new henchbugs, Number 1 and Number 2—formerly known as the Dung twins (no patent or anything, just saying).

All at once everybuggy exclaimed, "What're **YOU** doing here?"

"This diaper is my lair!" Crazy Cockroach declared.

Super Fly also spoke. "This diaper is our fortress of doody!"

"Find a new fortress!" commanded the king of the world.

Super Fly countered, "Why don't *you*?"

Fantastic Flea thought his friend looked extremely cool standing there in his cape. Would Crazy Cockroach be impressed enough to back down without a fight?

The roach slammed a fist powerful as a sledgehammer against one of the diaper's walls.

"Easy on the dojo!" Eugene exclaimed.

"We have just as much right to this diaper as you do," Fred added.

"Perhaps a game of rock, paper, scissors?" suggested one of the Dungs. "Best of three. Winner gets the lair."

"Deal," said the roach and fly at the same time.

Super Fly and Crazy Cockroach squared off and threw in their signs.

Rock. Rock.

Paper. Paper.

Scissors. Scissors.

This went on 3,650,673,937 more times. Each time it  was a tie. It was clear that this wouldn't be settled with a game.

Using 9,000 times the power of a regular cockroach, the super villain charged!

Eugene's enhanced reflexes allowed him

to zip out of the roach's way. Unfortunately, he smashed right into Fantastic Flea!

Poor Fred went tumbling over and over, into one of the diaper's soft, stinky walls. Meanwhile, the sheer speed of Super Fly's flight distracted Crazy Cockroach, causing him to crash into a pile of old bottle caps.

"Ouch!" Cornelius cried as he stumbled to his feet. The pleated metal edge of the cap scraped his exoskeleton. The cap wedged itself on the roach's head like a twisted metal crown.

Super Fly rushed to his sidekick's aid. "Are you okay?"

Fred did some stretches and paced around, like circus performers did when they got hurt. "A-okay!" Fred said.

Crazy Cockroach tried to pull the dented bottle cap off his head as he commanded, "Back to **MY** lair!"

Once they were alone on their side of the diaper, Eugene muttered, "We must find out what Crazy Cockroach and his poop-loving minions are planning."

Fred agreed, and the two quickly came up with a plan.

5

The Pizza Guy Is a Pizza Fly

Meanwhile, on the other side of the putrid diaper, Crazy Cockroach showed his hench-bugs his latest creation: a video game named *Butterfly Bombers*.

Number 1 and Number 2 looked skeptical. Wouldn't a real super villain invent a death ray, or at least something more menacing than a silly game?

"I designed it myself," Cornelius added proudly. Having crawled along at the bottom of his class from his first day of school, the roach enjoyed his new intellect, which had been enhanced 9,000 times.

The Dungs still didn't seem impressed.

"Why don't you try it?" Crazy Cockroach urged. The evil burning in his beady black eyes made the beetles readily agree.

"We'll play your game!" Number 1 exclaimed.

"What's it called again?" Number 2 asked.

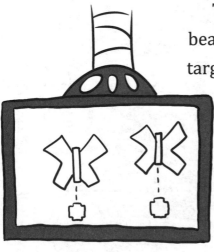

The goal was to fly beautiful butterflies over targets and drop brightly colored balls from above. The troubled twins had played many games. But none ever took hold of them like this. Their eyes locked on the screen with total focus.

They didn't even look up when someone pounded on the door to the lair. (After discovering his mortal foe's dojo was in the diaper's other leg, Cornelius had swiftly installed basic security, like a door.)

Crazy Cockroach expected his henchbugs to answer the door. But Numbers 1 and 2 continued to drop colored balls and swoop through rainbows on their brilliant wings.

Cornelius opened the door to find a pizza deliverybug. The fly wore a hat with the Best Pest Pizza logo on it, although the logo seemed to be cut out of a cardboard delivery carton. The T-shirt might have been drawn in marker.

"Best Pest Pizza," the delivery fly declared.

Crazy Cockroach glanced at his hypnotized henchbugs, then said, "No one here ordered a pizza. Maybe you're looking for Super Nerd next door."

Eugene struggled not to flinch at this insult. At least his improvised disguise worked despite the obvious flaws.

Then Cornelius looked thoughtful and asked, "Do I know you?"

Super Fly looked all around the lair. He used his super mental abilities to note every detail, every possible bit of information on the layout of this side of the diaper. The door had been a surprise. It was nice craftsmanship. It even had a peephole. What other security measures might his clever enemy have installed while he and Fred created this disguise?

As Super Fly took one last look around the

lair, Crazy Cockroach suddenly exclaimed, "Wait!"

Eugene froze. Was he busted? If the roach recognized him as Super Fly, would the super bully squash the fly flat like a fly swatter?

"Want to play a really great video game?" the cockroach asked.

Eugene blinked. This seemingly innocent invitation was the last thing Super Fly expected to hear.

He glanced at the dung beetles, still totally focused on the screen. Shifting colors of bursting butterfly bombs reflected in their black shells and hypnotized eyes.

Eugene felt tempted. The henchbugs seemed to be having such a great time! But he didn't want to push his luck with Cornelius. Besides, if he was gone much longer Fred would worry. Or worse, eat all the extra pizza they bought for this plan.

Super Fly recalled his disguise and quickly fibbed, "Maybe some other time. I've got pizzas to deliver."

"Well, let me give you a tip," Crazy Cockroach said, holding out something shiny in his hand. "Here's a nickel."

Eugene rolled his eyes. He'd heard roaches were lousy tippers!

Cornelius cackled. "Oh, wait, that's just a ring tab from a soda can."

The roach smiled one of his hideous smiles. Super Fly took the worthless ring and smiled back. "Thanks."

On the other side of the diaper, Fantastic Flea had indeed begun to worry and was almost done eating the extra-large pizza, just as Super Fly had suspected. He paced between the soft white walls like a caged beast.

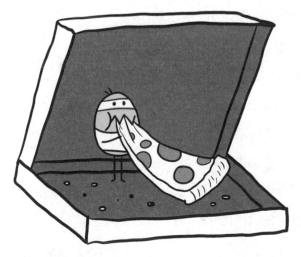

Fred turned and saw . . . Super Fly! The anxious flea asked his friend, "What did you learn?"

Super Fly described a drawing board covered with designs for a video game and a hot tub. Fred pictured the henchbugs playing the colorful video game in the luxurious lair filled with all the latest gadgets and gizmos . . .

"And even a Ping-Pong table!" Super Fly concluded.

Fred squealed, "**A PING- PONG TABLE!** How cool is their lair?"

"Calm down," Eugene told his friend.

He gestured to the other side of the diaper. Fred understood. It wasn't exactly good side-kicking to loudly praise the villain's lair.

Fred whispered, "What should we do? We need to know more."

The brilliant bug considered the situation. "We need to go back in." Then Eugene added, "By the way, Fred. You were right. Roaches are terrible tippers. Oh, and one more thing. You couldn't save me one lousy piece of pizza?"

The stuffed flea burped. "Sorry."

Super Fly tossed the ring tab up to the diaper's ceiling. Fantastic Flea flew through it and then turned a quick somersault before touching the absorbent floor.

6

Operation Super Spy

Fred's fabulous stunt gave Super Fly an idea. "I know how I can get back into Crazy Cockroach's lair unseen!"

"How?" The flea flipped a few times while waiting for his friend's reply. Before the hero could reveal his plan, his restless sidekick guessed, "Aren't you working on some kind of invisibility thing?"

Eugene looked down at his feet. The invisibility candy bar wasn't working out nearly as well as the key lime Ultimo 6-9000.

The chocolate tasted too chalky, and visibility still came and went at the most embarrassing times.

He didn't bother giving Fred this bad news. Instead, Super Fly announced grandly, "You're the only superpower we need for this job."

His loyal sidekick seemed skeptical. "You know I don't have any superpowers."

Super Fly smiled. "I believe in you. Now . . . doody calls!"

Moments later, Crazy Cockroach and his

henchbugs crawled out of their side of the diaper. Number 1 wondered, "What's making all that happy noise?"

Number 2 stared in amazement. He'd never seen a one-flea circus before. He didn't know any insect could move like that!

Fantastic Flea flipped and bounced, leaped and landed, all over the sand outside the dirty diaper. His act was even more mesmerizing than *Butterfly Bombers*! Even Crazy Cockroach couldn't take his eyes off the Fantastic Flea.

As Super Fly planned, he had no trouble sneaking into the lair behind them. Moving at super speed, the 9,000-times-enhanced fly searched desk drawers, file cabinets, and even the fridge.

Eugene paused for a moment of pure envy: his enemies even had a fridge! To cool off, he flew back and forth between each end of the Ping-Pong table so fast he played a hundred-point game against himself and won in less than fifteen seconds!

This performance was no more amazing than the one Fred gave outside the diaper.

Crazy Cockroach stared at the acrobatic bug. "Have we ever met?"

"Today?" asked the funny flea.

Meanwhile, Super Fly returned to his task. "So clever," he murmured as he looked at Crazy Cockroach's plans. "Of course, thanks to my Ultimo 6-9000, Cornelius is 9,000 times smarter than a normal roach." Eugene turned back to the video game plans. If Super Fly wasn't 9,000 times smarter than a smart fly, he might have missed the fact that those plans were for more than they seemed.

7

Crazy Cockroach Says!

As soon as Fred saw Eugene emerge from the diaper leg, he took his last bow. "Thanks, you've been a great audience."

Back in the other side of the diaper, Super Fly told Fantastic Flea, "That Crazy Cockroach is working on a video game he plans on using to take over the world!"

Fantastic Flea knew Crazy Cockroach was crazy, but taking over the world with a video game... "That sounds more nuts than an acorn-pie-eating contest for squirrels."

"Does that mean you think it's impossible?" Super Fly said. "Remember, Crazy Cockroach is super smart. Luckily, so am I!"

"Okay, if it's possible— how?" Fred asked.

Eugene wasn't sure. "The plan calls for gamers to become addicted to the game, then at some point in the program they become hypnotized. The roach hasn't figured out that part yet. But he's working on it."

Super Fly added, "From the way Dee and Doo ignored my first visit, we know he's managed to make the game addictive."

"We should stake out the other side of the diaper," suggested Fantastic Flea. "That way we'll know what these bad bugs are up to."

Then he added, "Are you sure that invisibility candy bar isn't ready for field testing?"

Eugene looked down at the fluffy-white floor. "Nothing wrong with a good old-fashioned stakeout!"

"I'll make some hot cocoa!" Fantastic Flea offered, adding, "If you go out for marshmallows."

Super Fly didn't mind. After all, it would take him less than two seconds to fly to Stinkmart.

Soon the pest friends sipped mallow-topped cocoa while perched on an old roller skate that gave them a great view of Crazy Cockroach's diaper entrance.

Eugene was about to add more marshmallows when the heroes suddenly saw movement outside the villain's lair.

Crazy Cockroach walked around the dump with the beetles trailing behind him. The bad bugs stopped at an old dirty shoe.

"Lick the shoe!" the roach commanded.

Number 1 and Number 2 licked the shoe.

"Did you see that?" Super Fly asked.

Fantastic Flea nodded. "Shoe lickers!"

Crazy Cockroach led his henchbugs around the dump, demanding they do one silly, gross, dangerous thing after another. Whatever the roach said, the Dungs did!

Fantastic Flea exclaimed, "It's like Simon Says, only now the game is Crazy Cockroach Says!"

Super Fly snapped to alarm. "This is no innocent game. Do you realize what this means?"

"That we should start having game night at our lair every Tuesday night?" replied the flea excitedly. "I can make s'mores."

"No. I mean, yes, that's a great idea. But no, this means something much bigger," replied the fly. "His plan is coming together!"

8

The Technology Trap

Alarm was the only logical conclusion. Fantastic Flea said, "If Crazy Cockroach really has created a game that will make players obey him like the Dungs are, Stinkopolis is in real trouble!"

Eugene saw the danger too. "You and I love video games. So do a lot of other bugs."

Fred agreed. "Almost every bug we know has a Bug Box gaming console."

But there wasn't anything the boys could

do about the super villain's plans that night. It was a school night, and they had homework.

While Eugene and Fred solved math problems, Cornelius was busy. As soon as our heroes entered Brown Barge Elementary School the next morning, they saw Number 1 and Number 2 passing out free video games to every bug.

Number 1 exclaimed, "This is the most awesome game you could imagine!"

Number 2 added, "And it's absolutely free!"

Number 1 continued the pitch. "Bug Box

compatible and will provide an exciting adventure for any bug!"

Fred accepted one of the colorful video game boxes.

"What are you doing?" Eugene asked.

"We won't know what it does unless we play it," Fred said.

Eugene realized his friend was right. So he took a free video game too.

Then he heard Cornelius C. Roach's voice behind him. "Give him one for his little sister too." And the Dungs did just that.

Free or not, Super Fly had no intention of giving that villain's game to Elle. So while Fred played *Butterfly Bombers* for several hours, Eugene studied Elle's copy under a microscope.

Eugene worked so long he forgot his friend was still in the diaper. "Didn't you go home?" he asked. Fred did not answer. He just kept dropping colorful bombs as he  swooped through a rainbow with his brilliant wings.

Eugene looked at the clock. Fred had played for seven hours straight!

Super Fly offered his sidekick "Cocoa? Marshmallows? A quick trip to the moon?"

Fred never took his eyes off the screen. Super Fly sighed. This could be a problem.

9

King of the School

The next day, Brown Barge Elementary buzzed with news of a special election.

"Vote for Cornelius!" cried Adam Aphid.

"Root for the roach!" chanted Grace Grasshopper.

An ant named Andy exclaimed, "Let's make Cornelius C. Roach student-body president!"

The gathered bugs cheered.

Eugene felt stunned. "We already have a student-body president!"

Super Fly waited for common sense to win.

Instead, Fred said, "Vote for Cornelius!"

During lunch, Fred tried to explain his sudden desire to elect the Crazy Cockroach. "I just feel this impulse to glorify Cornelius C. Roach. He's such a worthy bug. I know he'd be the greatest student-body president ever!" the flea gushed.

By the time the final bell rang, Cornelius had been voted president of Brown Barge Elementary! Elle fumed, "How can a whole school full of bugs forget all the misery that bully caused? How can everyone suddenly like such a cruel cockroach?"

10

Cornelius for Mayor

Each day Number 1 and Number 2 brought more and more *Butterfly Bombers* games to give out for free. By Monday morning every bug at Brown Barge Elementary—every student, teacher, and administrator—had played the amazing video game. Even the janitor hid in the maintenance closet and played all day long, causing an unfortunate shortage of toilet paper in the bathrooms.

Butterfly Bombers was all anyone talked about. In history, students learned about bombs. In art class, they painted butter-flies. In gym, they practiced flying—even the bugs that didn't have wings!

As far as they knew, Elle and Eugene were the only bugs that hadn't played it yet. Poor Fred couldn't pull himself away!

"I'm fine," he told Eugene. "I just love the game; that's all. It's so much cooler than *Sewer Invaders*. I'm already on level three."

Elle groaned. "Big deal. You've been playing it nonstop!"

Eugene added, "Don't you realize you're letting our enemy hypnotize you?"

Fred shrugged. "Cornelius isn't so bad. Why hold his past against him? The roach has become really nice lately."

Eugene and Elle had both noticed that Cornelius no longer bullied the smaller bugs at Brown Barge. Instead, everyone just gave him whatever he wanted.

"Take my lunch, please," offered Andy.

Eugene stared. Andy was one hungry ant. And now he was happily donating his tray full of food to the cockroach?

"Here, I did your homework for you, Cornelius," said Charlie Cricket.

Mrs. Tiger Moth gave Cornelius As on all his assignments just for putting his name on his paper.

In gym class, Coach Caterpillar made the roach captain of the football team.

Eugene raised his feeler. "Um, Coach, Cornelius doesn't even play football."

Coach Caterpillar replied, "He does now!"

Coach was gone, just like the rest of the adults. Crazy Cockroach wanted to turn

Stinkopolis into his own playground. The fate of the whole dump—and the world—now rested on the wings of one superhero and his plucky little sister.

Eugene invited Elle to join him in the dirty diaper. "This place is cool!" she exclaimed. "Could use a Ping-Pong table and maybe a fridge," she added.

Eugene sighed. "Kind of a sore point. Why don't we focus on finding a solution to the hypnosis?"

Elle suggested, "Let's try chanting spell-breaking sayings, like *abracadabra wallack-ajam, candied yam, beaver dam!*"

"Nonsense. We need science!" Eugene exclaimed. Using Fred as a subject, he tried several methods of ending the hypnotic state.

Elle wasn't impressed. "Why would jumping jacks work?"

Eugene panted. "Fred loves jumping

jacks. I thought if I started he'd join in and try to beat me."

At school, Elle tried clapping right in front of her hypnotized friends' eyes. Everyone just laughed at her.

Adele Aphid swore, "We all like Cornelius because he's cool!"

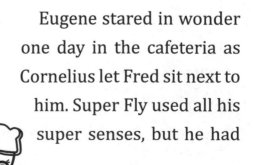

Eugene stared in wonder one day in the cafeteria as Cornelius let Fred sit next to him. Super Fly used all his super senses, but he had to admit Crazy Cockroach didn't do any-thing suspicious, unless you count sharing his scab sandwich.

Fred said, "Maybe nothing's going on. Maybe the bully bug just got tired of being nasty."

After school, instead of practicing super-hero moves, playing *Sewer Invaders*, or oth-erwise hanging out, Fred went home. Super Fly felt as if he'd lost his pest friend.

That night on TV, Eugene and Elle saw a new commercial. It featured the horribly

smiling face of Brown Barge Elementary's worst bully. The siblings turned to each other in horror and exclaimed in unison, "Cornelius for mayor?"

Elle scoffed. "A fourth grader can't get elected. And how does an elementary school kid pay for a TV commercial?"

"From years of stealing lunch money!" Eugene replied.

Super Fly sensed the fiend's plan was possible. "Today student council president, tomorrow mayor of Stinkopolis, and by Tuesday . . ."

Super Fly suddenly knew what Crazy Cockroach wanted. He knew what all the plans on the drawing board meant.

Eugene announced, "Cornelius is taking over the world—not with an army of robots, but with brainwashing! He's creating an army of zombies to do his bidding!"

11

Roach Domination

Super Fly flew next door to confront Cornelius. Hogging half the dirty diaper was bad enough. But taking over the world . . . that was going too far!

Crazy Cockroach grinned, laughing maniacally. "You'll never be able to prove it! Besides, it's too late. I'm getting orders from all over the world for my new *Butterfly Bombers* game. It's spreading faster than a fire in a greasy diner."

The royal roach finally ended his rant,

"Soon enough they'll make me king bug of the earth!"

Crazy Cockroach opened the door to show Super Fly his pest friend sitting with Number 1 and Number 2 in front of a Bug Box, playing *Butterfly Bombers*. If this fiendish super roach could turn Fred against the cause of insect justice . . .

Super Fly did the only thing a hero could do. He offered, "Let's end this once and for all; bug against bug, fly against roach."

Crazy Cockroach laughed in his face. Super Fly could smell the rancid cottage cheese he'd had for lunch.

"I outsmarted you!" Cornelius cackled. "I beat you with my superior brain! Don't be a sore loser!"

For the first time since he'd become Super Fly, Eugene felt deeply afraid. Was Cornelius's brain really superior? Could Super Fly defeat the villain again—or would Stinkopolis and the world fall?

Eugene felt very alone. This was the kind of moment when Fantastic Flea would say something encouraging, or at least confusing.

Super Fly suddenly knew that without his sidekick, he couldn't defeat Crazy Cockroach. Eugene had to find some way to get Fred back and end that rotten roach's reign once and for all!

After a fortifying supper of prime poo, Super Fly felt inspired, energized, and ready for the quest. Then something horrible happened.

Before searching for a way to save his sidekick, Eugene planned to say good night to his little sister. Elle didn't answer his knock.

Eugene knocked again. Had she fallen

asleep? He knocked a third time before turning the knob. Colored lights flickered in one corner of the room. Elle was staring at a screen full of beautiful butterflies.

Super Fly screamed, "Nooooooo! Not Elle! Not Elle too!"

12

The Big Contest

Eugene knew science. He also knew cartoons. And he knew that sometimes the only way to beat someone is to join them in whatever it is they're doing.

So Super Fly devoted his brilliant brain to creating his own video game to break the roach's spell. Thanks to being 9,000 times more

brilliant than the average fly (really ought to patent the Ultimo!), Eugene took only one night to devise a game so great and so addictive that it would be even more *gotta-play* than *Butterfly Bombers*.

At dawn, Eugene ran one final test on his masterpiece: *Roach Raid*. The new game was Bug Box ready, and his new plan would soon unfold!

Before the first bell, the halls of Brown Barge Elementary School always swarmed with bugs. Eugene addressed the crowd, inviting them all to a video-game contest after school the following day.

He posted flyers all over Stinkopolis. Soon everyone was talking about "the biggest event at the dump in years!"

Since the whole town had been dropping

big butterfly bombs lately, they expected to play Cornelius's game. Instead, Eugene gave every bug a copy of *Roach Raid*.

As soon as the final bell rang, the whole school started walking, crawling, creeping, and flying down to the dump.

Super Fly couldn't believe his multifaceted eyes. It seemed like every bug in Stinkopolis had gathered by the thousands. Kids, parents, teachers, police bugs, fire bugs, big and little, parasites and queen bees.

So far, so good! Eugene spotted Fred among the video-game zombies playing *Butterfly Bombers* over and over.

Super Fly's plan had only one problem. No one would stop playing *Butterfly Bombers* long enough to even try *Roach Raid*!

Eugene glanced at one zombie's log-on screen: 100,000 bugs were flapping their digital wings at the whim of that crazy roach.

Just then Cornelius emerged from a

hidden cave perched high atop the dump. He returned to the dump dressed as Crazy Cockroach.

Eugene knew it was time to turn into Super Fly! Shedding his glasses and putting on his stain-resistant cape, Eugene became a hero 9,000 times more amazing than the average fly.

He flew straight for Crazy Cockroach! But before Super Fly could land a blow, Cornelius commanded his 100,000 players to "**ATTACK!**"

Super Fly considered the obedient swarm. He was worse than outnumbered: he was 91,000 bugs short of a fair fight!

If ever a hero needed a sidekick, Super Fly sure needed Fred. But like most of Stinkopolis, Fred had turned into a video zombie, and Elle was nowhere to be found!

Eugene wanted to find his little sister and save his friend, but first he had to fight off a horde of hypnotized bees and wasps! Stingers poked and stabbed. Super Fly was fast, but speed was no match for the cruel hunters. Swollen with poison, Super Fly finally passed out.

Crazy Cockroach had devised the perfect deathtrap for his enemy. Zombie bugs placed poor Super Fly on a giant piece of sticky flypaper. The flypaper floated atop a lily pad in the middle of the murky pond at the end of the dump. How long before Super Fly became a hungry frog's tasty treat?

While the hero lay helpless, the villain's

zombie empire grew. Each moment, more and more bugs became addicted to *Butterfly Bombers*. Crazy Cockroach watched the number of log-ons grow. Soon . . . soon . . . all the bugs would be hooked on dropping pretty colors, and he would control the world!

13

Fly Girl

Since Elle was even more stubborn than the average little sister, she had enough will-power to resist the beautiful butterflies. (That—and because Mom made her "shut that noisy thing off.")

Realizing she was hungry, Elle opened the fridge and looked straight at the slice of key lime pie covered in warning signs.

Now she was both

hungry and curious. Having added up all the clues, Elle guessed this pie (the Ultimo 6-9000, Patent 1234555, filed with the United Insects Patent Office) had caused her brother to become the superhero known as Super Fly.

She figured this tasty dessert would either transform her into a superhero . . . or at the very least make a nice snack. Since Eugene wasn't around to stop her, Elle took a bite of the precious pastry!

Within six seconds, the second grader was 9,000 times smarter, faster, better at everything. Elle had suddenly become the superhero known as **FLY GIRL!**

Elle had read enough of Eugene's comics to know

that powers alone couldn't make a hero. She needed . . . a super awesome outfit!

Elle always had a keen fashion sense. So it didn't take her long to pull together something that said cool, capable, and I make this cape look good. Fly Girl was . . . fly!

Name, check. Outfit, check. Elle didn't hesitate to decide on Fly Girl's first mission. She had to save her brother! With 9,000 times her usual intuition, Elle suddenly knew exactly where to find Eugene.

Fly Girl flew to the murky pond 9,000 times faster than she'd ever flown before. And a good thing too, because she found Super Fly surrounded by 101 frogs eager to make a meal of him.

Weak, dizzy, and swollen

from all those wasp and hornet stings, Super Fly simply couldn't break free from the flypaper! The helpless hero wondered, "Is this the end of Super Fly?"

Then something almost faster than he could see swooped over the lily pad.

SQUISH! SLOSH! PLOP! Frogs flopped everywhere as Fly Girl flew down to rescue Eugene. Elle carried him off just before a giant bullfrog could snag Super Fly with his long tongue.

Eugene didn't need to be 9,000 times smarter to recognize Elle. "You're . . ."

"A superhero!" his sister squealed. "Isn't it great?"

Eugene looked down at the angry bullfrog. "I guess so. And I guess you ate a certain patented piece of pie."

Fly Girl grinned.

14

Reverse Engineering

The two flew back to the dirty diaper to plan their next move. Eugene felt frustrated. "If only those zombies had played one round of *Roach Raid*. It's ten times as addictive as *Butterfly Bombers*."

"Let that go," Elle said. "We just have to think of another way to reverse the hypnosis . . ." Elle's voice trailed off. "What if we reverse the programming, somehow get *Butterfly Bombers* to play backward, at least the part that's casting this zombie spell."

Super Fly had to admit Fly Girl's idea had merit. As the only two bugs in all of Stinkopolis who hadn't spent the majority of the recent past staring at a screen with vacant, obedient eyes, the super siblings didn't have too many options.

"I think I know how to reverse the programming of the game," Eugene began. "But how can we break into Crazy Cockroach's lair a third time without making him suspicious?"

Eugene didn't want to risk wearing the Pest Pizza delivery hat and T-shirt again.

Elle suggested a different disguise. She returned from her room wearing her Insect

Scout uniform. "No one can resist our stink patties."

It was true! Eugene's mouth parts watered just at the thought of those gooey, gross cookies. They were disgustingly delicious. He hated to put his little sister in danger, but Eugene reminded himself of two things. Not only was Elle getting to be a big bug now, she was also Fly Girl!

Ding-dong. Crazy Cockroach no longer expected his henchbugs to answer the diaper's door. Number 1 and Number 2 were as hooked on *Butterfly Bombers* as their companion, Fred.

Cornelius opened the door, and Elle greeted him, "Insect Scout Cookies for sale.

All the most repulsive flavors! Who can resist Used Toilet Paper Twist? Can I put you down for a dozen boxes of the Snot-Covered Dung Drops?"

Elle expertly continued the pitch while peering farther into the diaper.

There sat Fred, still mindlessly dropping digital color bombs. He wasn't leaping or flipping or babbling or Fredding at all!

Elle couldn't care much about the Dungs. They had been brainless zombies long before the video game existed.

Crazy Cockroach wouldn't commit to buying a dozen boxes of cookies. "That's too much. I have to watch my abdomen." He changed the subject. "Would you like to play a video game?"

The Insect Scout hesitated. Cornelius stared at her. "You look familiar . . ."

Elle quickly said, "We flies all look alike." Then she added, "No thanks, I'm not really into video games. Gotta fly! Bye-bye." The Insect Scout left, and the second part of the Flysteins' plan began.

When his doorbell rang again, Crazy Cockroach was surprised to see Super Fly! Cornelius blinked in disbelief. "Why aren't you at the pond feeding the frogs?"

Eugene boasted, "Because not even the Ultimo 6-9000 (an invention worthy of every possible legal protection) could make you smart enough to beat the super-sly Super Fly!"

Crazy Cockroach laughed. "I'm 9,000 times the bug you'll ever be!"

"In about six seconds you'll be history," Eugene blustered. "And not the kind of history that inspires books, movies, monuments, and collectibles. I mean the kind of dusty old history that everyone forgets."

Cornelius replied, "Do you really think no one will recall my attempt to take over the world with giant robots?" Then he handed Eugene a cup as he smirked, "Can I offer you a Crazy Cockroach calendar, T-shirt, key chain, or coffee mug?"

"No thanks! I'm too young to drink coffee." Eugene continued, "Besides, it's not like you really accomplished anything."

Super Fly continued taunting the villain to give Elle time to change from her Insect Scout clothes into her Fly Girl outfit and to reprogram the game on Crazy Cockroach's computer. Before they'd left, Eugene had figured out which keys to tap to reverse the game's hypnotic effect.

Fly Girl quickly performed the complex sequence of keystrokes. Super Fly felt very proud of her.

Meanwhile, Crazy Cockroach became more annoyed with his enemy's pointless banter. "I never should've left you to die in that deathtrap," Cornelius moaned. "I should've learned from all those TV shows. Why does the villain leave the hero to escape? Lazy, careless . . . Why can't I be more thorough?"

Fly Girl gave her brother the OK signal. Eugene shrugged. "Who knows? Maybe villains are just born slackers."

Before Cornelius could reply, all three

bugs reacted to a scuffle coming from the back part of the diaper.

"What're you doing here?" Number 1 shouted.

"Get that stupid flea!" Number 2 exclaimed.

"I'm not stupid; I'm Fred!"

BAM! SLAM! BOOM! The two hench-bugs and Fred continued fighting.

Elle grinned. All three had stopped playing *Butterfly Bombers*. That meant the reversal had worked!

Cornelius rushed to see what was

happening. "Who are you?" he asked as his eyes fell on the nicely dressed new superhero.

"I'm Fly Girl, and your plan is foiled," Elle announced.

"Ridiculous!" Crazy Cockroach asserted. But it was true!

Not only had his henchbugs and Fred emerged from their trance, but all over Earth, bugs had stopped playing the roach's game. No longer hypnotized, they'd gone back to their normal lives.

Crazy Cockroach still could not accept his defeat. "Lick my shoes!" he commanded.

The Dung twins and Fred stared at the roach.

"Lick your own shoes," Dee replied.

"I'm not hungry," Doo added.

"Fleas don't lick shoes," Fred said.

Crazy Cockroach became even more furious than usual. He pressed a button on his remote control that locked his lair with giant steel bolts. The flies and flea were trapped.

15

Three on Three

Crazy Cockroach and his henchbugs attacked! Super Fly and Fly Girl struggled to fend them off. Then suddenly the heroes and villains heard a knock at the door.

Cornelius wondered who it could be. The diaper wasn't usually this busy.

He unlocked the steel bolts

and flung the door open wide, but no one was there.

Under the table, Fred chuckled to himself. He'd been knocking on the underside of the table to fool the fiend! The 9,000-times-smarter roach had just fallen for the oldest trick in the book.

As Crazy Cockroach came back inside to resume fighting, Fred bounced out the door over the roach's head. He ran to the Fortress of Doody to transform into Fantastic Flea.

With Fred now in his super suit, even though he technically didn't have super-powers, the fight became a fair three against three.

But Cornelius wasn't happy. He moaned, "You're destroying my lair!"

No one cared. They were too busy throwing punches and dodging kicks. With a mighty grunt, Number 2 tossed Fred through the wall into the other side of the diaper.

Now it was Super Fly's turn to fuss. "Oh no! You're wrecking our Fortress of Doody!"

But still the fighting went on and on for hours, until both sides were exhausted and both lairs ruined. The only thing that remained intact was the Ping-Pong table. And that gave Super Fly an idea.

"Let's settle this over a game of Ping-Pong," he suggested. "If I win, Crazy Cockroach will stop trying to take over the world. And if you win, I agree not to stop your evil plans."

Cornelius cackled. "Ping-Pong? I will destroy you in Ping-Pong. I've never lost a game."

"First to twenty-one wins," Super Fly said.

The two bugs shook on it, and the game began.

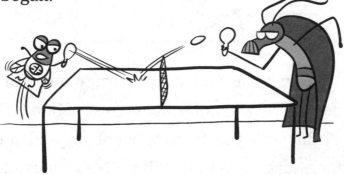

Since both bugs were 9,000 times faster than ordinary insects, the ball flew across the table so fast it became almost invisible. Crazy Cockroach won the first point, but Super Fly took the second.

And so it went. Crazy Cockroach seized the lead, then Super Fly, then Crazy Cockroach again, and so on, until suspense hung like a fart inside the diaper and the score was twenty to twenty.

"Come on, Eugene!" Elle cheered.

Super Fly hit the tiny white ball so fast Fantastic Flea almost didn't see it. Had the hero missed? No! Crazy Cockroach had swung his paddle but . . . the ball flew past it!

Super Fly jumped up and screamed, "I **WON!**"

Fantastic Flea and Fly Girl rushed up to him. Fred waved one of his forelegs and exclaimed, "High flyve!" Eugene was happy to return their special salute.

Crazy Cockroach threw his paddle on the floor. But thanks to its soft, absorbent

padding, the paddle just bounced. So the furious bully smashed it over his henchbugs' heads.

Number 1 protested, "Hey, what did we do?"

Number 2 added, "You're the one who lost!"

That only made Cornelius angrier, so the smashing continued, and the losing team proceeded to beat each other up.

Super Fly suggested, "Let's go home."

Fly Girl agreed.

Fantastic Flea added, "Maybe we can start looking for a bigger lair now that our team has three members, not just two."

Elle grinned.

Super Fly looked thoughtful. "I wonder who we'll be fighting now that Crazy Cockroach has promised to stop trying to take over the world."

Later that night, Eugene heard a knock on his window. When he went to open it, no one was there. But he found a strange note left behind.

Dear Eugene—I mean, Super Fly:

Sucker! I had my fingers crossed the whole time!
You didn't really think I was going to stop trying to take over the world, did you?
I'm going to destroy the world with even more vengeance now!

Sincerely,

Cornelius—I mean, Crazy Cockroach

P.S. I want a rematch!

Todd H. Doodler is the author and illustrator of the Super Fly series, *Rawr!* and the Bear in Underwear series, as well as many other fun books for young readers. He is also the founder of David & Goliath, a humorous T-shirt company, and Tighty Whitey Toys, which makes plush animals in underwear. He, too, is a part-time superhero and lives in Los Angeles with his daughter, Elle, and their two labradoodles, Muppet and Pickleberry.